29

Joe Mathieu

THE
SESAME STREET®
LIBRARY

With Jim Henson's Muppets

VOLUME 8

FEATURING
THE LETTERS
Q AND R
AND THE NUMBER
8

Children's Television Workshop/Funk & Wagnalls, Inc.

WRITTEN BY:

Michael Frith
Jerry Juhl
Emily Perl Kingsley
Sharon Lerner
Nina B. Link
Albert G. Miller
Jeffrey Moss
Norman Stiles
Jon Stone
Daniel Wilcox

ILLUSTRATED BY:

Mel Crawford
A. Delaney
Mary Lou Dettmer
Michael Frith
David Gantz
Joseph Mathieu
Marc Nadel
Kelly Oechsli
Michael J. Smollin
Kay Wood

PHOTOGRAPHS BY:

Charles P. Rowan

0-8343-0016-8   3 4 5 6 7 8 9 0

ERNIE PRESENTS
THE LETTER Q

ERNIE DUSTS THE SHELF

One morning when Bert returned home from the store,
He found Ernie mumbling and walking the floor.
"What's wrong with you, Ernie, old buddy?" he said,
"How come you are talking and scratching your head?"

"There's something," said Ernie, "that I have forgotten.
Forgetting it makes me feel stupid and rotten.
It's something that I've got to do for myself
Before I start dusting this toy-covered shelf."

"This toy shelf," Bert snorted, "needs plenty of dusting.
The way you are stalling is simply disgusting!
Just look at the dirt on your poor rubber duckie.
He's dusty, he's grimy, he's filthy, he's *yucchy!*"

"I'm really not stalling," said Ernie. "It's *true*
That I can't remember the thing I must do
Before the dust-up of the shelf has begun.
I *know* it's important. It *has* to be done."

"Get busy, you meatball!" Bert shouted. "You *must!*
Quit stalling! Start working! Get rid of that dust!"
"Okay," Ernie said, "if you say so, I'll do it.
I'll skip what I had to do first and get to it!"

He rushed to the shelf, and with one mighty sweep
He whisked all the toys to the floor in a heap,
And though some were bent and broken and shattered,
The shelf was now clean and that's all that mattered.

Poor Bert pointed down to the toys at their feet.
"You birdbrain!" he hollered. "Good gosh! Holy Pete!
You're cuckoo! Bananas! Your brain must be busting!
Why didn't you take the toys *off* before dusting?"

"That's *it!*" shouted Ernie, just jumping for joy.
"Hey, thanks for reminding me, old buddy boy.
You take the toys *off* before dusting the shelf!
That's what I was trying to think of my*self!*"

As Bert knocked his head on the edge of the bed,
Ernie picked up his dear duckie and said,
"I'm happy that I was reminded by Bert,
But happier still that my duckie's not hurt."

Qq

The Queer Question Quiz

Hi, everybody.

Guy Smiley here to bring you the moment
you've all been waiting for—the Queer Question Quiz!
Ladies and gentlemen, I hope you noticed that the words
"Queer Question Quiz" all begin with the letter Q. Now, before
I ask you today's Queer Question, I want to give you a clue
to the answer. Today's answer has a whole lot of Q words in it.
And now, here it is, folks—the moment you've all been
waiting for—today's Queer Question on the Queer
Question Quiz. Today's Queer Question is:

WHAT DID FARMER QUINCY SAY TO HIS PET DUCK
QUEENIE WHEN HE WANTED HER TO
STOP MAKING NOISE?

Take your time, think it over. . . . Okay, folks, your time is up! The answer to today's Queer Question Quiz is:
Farmer Quincy said to his pet duck . . .
QUACK
QUACK QUACK QUACK
QUIT QUACKING QUICK, QUEENIE, AND KEEP QUIET!
QUACK
Look at all those Q words in one sentence, folks! If that's not enough for you, try saying it five times fast. In the meantime, this is Guy Smiley saying "so long for now" from the Queer Question Quiz! See you again soon. And now, on with the book. . . .
QUACK
QUACK
QUACK
QUACK
J. Mathieu

Hansel and Gretel

Hansel and Gretel were walking in the woods. Their stepmother had told them to gather firewood, but instead they watched the birds and chased after butterflies. All at once they realized they didn't know where they were.

The two children were very frightened. But since they could not find their way home, they had to spend the night in the woods.

The next morning they saw a beautiful little house nearby. "Look! It's made of gingerbread!" cried Gretel.

They were so hungry they began to break little bits off the doorway and gobble them up.

Suddenly they heard a strange voice. "Nibble, nibble like a mouse. Who is nibbling at my house?"

And the wicked old witch who lived there jumped out and grabbed them. She locked Hansel in a cage. "I'll eat you when you're a little fatter," she said. Then she told Gretel to light the oven fire for supper.

But Gretel was a clever girl. "Show me how," she said.

"You silly goose," scolded the witch. "This is how it's done." The old woman leaned into the oven and lit the fire. Quick as a wink, Gretel pushed her into the oven. The old witch disappeared in a puff of smoke.

Then Gretel let Hansel out of the cage, and they ran away as fast as they could.

King Hungry the Eighth

King Hungry the Eighth
ordered dinner one day.
He called for his cooks
to appear right away.
"I'm hungry," he said,
"so bring me my plate,
and make sure the things on it
all number **8**!"

They brought him **8** hot dogs and **8** toasted rolls,
8 pickles, **8** pretzels, **8** donuts with holes.

The King ate them all and he wiped off his chin,
and smiled and said, "Not a bad way to begin."

"Now bring me," the King said, "**8** French fried potatoes.
And **8** lemon pies with **8** juicy tomatoes."

He swallowed it all with **8** pieces of bread.
"I'm not called King Hungry for nothing!" he said.

So they brought him **8** pizzas
with sausage and cheese,
and the King gulped them down
just as quick as you please.

Then he gobbled **8** turkeys
with stuffing and yams,
and **8** black-eyed peas,
and then **8** boiled hams.

Said the King to the cooks, "My, but eating is fun!"
Now bring me dessert so my meal will be done!"

For dessert the King polished off
8 chocolate cakes…

And went off to bed
with **8** *big tummy-aches!!*

The Monsters' Picnic

Herry, Cookie and Grover
are going UP the hill
to have a picnic.

Herry is playing UP in the tree.
Cookie and Grover are DOWN on the ground.
Herry is OVER Grover. . .

. . .and—Oops!—Grover
is UNDER Herry.

The monsters are sitting AROUND
the picnic blanket. They are
ready to have their picnic.

Hortense is IN the picnic basket.
The picnic is IN Hortense.

The picnic blanket is IN Herry.
The picnic basket is IN Cookie.
Grover is going DOWN the hill to buy a hot dog.

Rr

Big Bird's Ridiculous Rhinoceros Rhymes

Little Jack Horner
Sat in a corner,
Eating his Christmas pie.
He stuck in his thumb
And pulled out . . .
a RHINOCEROS!

Hickory, Dickory, Dock,
The RHINOCEROS
Ran up the clock.

There was an old woman
Who lived in a shoe.
She had so many
RHINOCEROSES
She didn't know what to do.

Sing a song of sixpence,
A pocket full of
RHINOCEROSES!

Old Mother Hubbard went
to the cupboard
To get her poor dog a bone.
But when she got there, she found . . .
a RHINOCEROS!

Ridiculous Rhinoceros Rhymes
may be silly, but RHINOCEROS
begins with the letter R, and
that's what's really important.

Old Mother Hubbard
Went to the cupboard
To give her poor dog a bone.
But when she got there,
The cupboard was bare
And so the poor dog had none.

Ernie and Bert's Counting Story

7 airplanes

8 saddle shoes

Cookie Monster's Colored Candy Cookies

Oh, boy! Me got a good one for you this time! COLORED CANDY COOKIES! They not only *delicious*, they *beautiful*, too! For this one you need:

1. Your COOKIE DOUGH! If you no have some in icebox, make some QUICK! (See Volume 1.)

2. Some lollipops or hard candies. Find some pretty colored ones.

3. Hammer (or something to break up candies with).

4. Tin foil.

Cover cookie sheet with tin foil. Sprinkle flour on cloth. Roll out dough on cloth (about ¼ inch thick) and cut into thin strips. Now use strips of dough to make pictures on tin foil, like this . . .

Now break up colored candies into little pieces and put pieces in openings in your pictures, like this . . .

Heat oven to 400 degrees. Now bake 6 to 8 minutes. While me wait, me play Roosevelt Franklin's favorite game. Hmmm. Me look around, and guess what me found. It something RED and . . . TASTY—

COOK BOOK!

REMEMBER! Never use oven without grown-up helping you.

O.K. COOKIES READY!

If you want to make beautiful COOKIE-POPS, put sticks in while still hot. Then let cool and peel off tin foil when hard. Oh, they ALMOST too pretty to eat.

But not quite!

Cookie and the Count LOVE the Baker

Old King Cole was a merry old soul
And a merry old soul was he.

He called for his pipe, and he called for his bowl,
And he called for his fiddlers three.

Ernie's Guessing Game

When I Grow Up
by Big Bird

When I grow up I'll drive a bus—
I'll let you honk the horn.
Or I could be a grocer—
And I'd sell peas and corn.

Or I could be a teacher—
I bet you'd learn a lot—
No, I think I'll be... a DANCER!
Oops—I think I'd better not.

On second thought, a carpenter
Is what I'd like the best—
I'd take a hammer, nails, and wood
And build a brand new nest.

Or... I could be a doctor—
And I'd make you feel all better.
Or I could be a mailman—
And I'd bring you a letter.

There are so many things to be—
It's really hard to choose.
But while I'm waiting to grow up...
I think I'll take a snooze.

Hello, everybodee! This is your old friend, Grover, flying up in the sky in my little pink airplane.

The sky is a good place to be to talk to you about the words **ABOVE** and **BELOW**. I will fly down a little lower and explain what I mean.

See those trees down there? I, Grover, am **ABOVE** the trees. The trees are **BELOW** me.

Now I will fly higher and then I will talk to you some more.

I am much higher now! I am up close to the fluffy white clouds. This cloud is **ABOVE** me. The ground is down **BELOW** me.

Now look out!
Up I go, even *higher!*

Here I am—furry, lovable old Grover—flying closer to the hot, yellow sun. The sun is **ABOVE** me. And I am **BELOW** the sun.

Now I am going to fly higher *still!*

I am **ABOVE** you. You are so far **BELOW** me you cannot even see me.

Okay now, fasten your seat belts! We are going down for a landing.

The ground is **BELOW** me, and that is where I am going to land. OOPS! I, Grover, am flying too *fast* in my little airplane.

Next time, I do not think that I, Grover, will talk to you about **ABOVE** and **BELOW**. Next time, I will talk about the lovely word **ON** . . . like **ON** the ground. After this, that is where I think I am going to stay.

A GROUCH-O-PHONE!

A Very Old Shape Story

One day, a very long time ago, a cave man was pulling a box of rocks. "This rock box is so hard to pull," the cave man complained, "that by the time I get to my rock garden I'm too tired to do anything."

Then the cave man had a terrific idea. "I'll put some things under the rock box to make it roll," he shouted out.

He went to his cave. Since triangles were his favorite shape, he decided to use triangles. After many hours of hard work, the cave man had hammered out four stone triangles. He attached them to his rock box and began to pull. Because the triangles had three corners, they couldn't roll.

He pulled

and pulled...

until...

the rope broke.

"I really do love triangles, but maybe I'd better use squares instead," he thought to himself. So he went back to the cave and hammered out four stone squares.

He attached them to his rock box and pulled. The squares were even harder to pull than the triangles because they had four corners. Again the rope broke.

"I guess this wasn't such a hot idea," the cave man mumbled as he kicked a big round rock sitting in his path. The round rock began to roll down the hill.

"Round!" the cave man yelled. "Why didn't I think of that before?"

So he hurried home and hammered out four round stones. When he attached them to his rock box the round stones rolled smoothly along because they didn't have any corners.

Pretty soon all his neighbors wanted round stones for their rock boxes, too, so the cave man opened up a Round Stone Shop in his cave. "I think I'll call these round stones...*bananas*," the cave man announced—and so he did.

The End

Big Bird's COLORS

GREEN is the color of Granny Bird's couch,
of grass and of spinach and Oscar the Grouch.

It's not easy being green.

Cookie and Grover and Herry are **BLUE**,
and bluebirds and bluebells
and blueberries, too.

Do you prefer the gold or silver trim?

This flower is **PURPLE** and so are these grapes,
and so are ALL of Prince Charming's fine capes.

RED is tomatoes, stoplights and cherries,
and strawberry jam— and that necktie of Herry's!

An orange is **ORANGE**
and so is Bert's nose—
and Ernie is orange—and so are my toes.

YELLOW bananas—and a big bumblebee,
and daisies and butter
—and don't forget ME!

THE BOY, THE GIRL AND THE JELLYBEANS

CHAPTER ONE

One day a boy was skipping merrily down the street, talking happily to himself.

"Boy, am I happy!" he whooped. "I've got a bag stuffed with jellybeans! And I'm crazy about jellybeans! I *love* jellybeans!"

Suddenly, the boy heard a girl crying. "Hey, girl," the boy said, "how come you're crying?"

"I'm crying because I'm sad," the girl moaned. "I'm *really* unhappy."

"That's strange," said the boy. "I'm feeling great! What's wrong?"

The girl wiped away a knuckleful of tears. "I lost my jellybeans," she sobbed. "That's what's wrong. And jellybeans are just wonderful. Did you ever lose *your* jellybeans?"

"Lose my jellybeans!" yelled the boy. "You must be bananas!"

"Then you can't know how I feel," she wept. "You would have to lose *your* jellybeans to know how sad I am."

"Wait a second," said the boy.
"I've got a whole bag full of
jellybeans here."

"You have?" said the girl.

"I sure have! And do you know
what? I'm feeling *so* happy and *so*
good, maybe I'll give them to you."

"You will?" she yelled. "Oh joy!"

"Yes, yes, I will! I will! Here, take
them! Take them! Take the whole bag!"

The girl grabbed the bag. "Hey," she shrieked happily. "This is fantastic! I've got jellybeans! I feel great! Wonderful! HAPPY! Thanks a lot, boy." And clutching the bag of jellybeans, she ran off down the street.

"Wow!" the boy said, really pleased with himself. "I sure am pleased with myself. I really cheered her up by giving her my jellybeans. Hey, wait just a minute!" he cried. "I loved my jellybeans. I adored my jellybeans! But I gave my jellybeans away! *Oh no!* How could I do it?"

The boy burst into tears. "Oh, am I SAD!" he bawled. "Oh, am I UNHAPPY!" he sobbed. "Other people could never know how sad I am. Unless," he sniffled, "they'd lost *their* jellybeans, too . . ."

TO BE CONTINUED IN VOLUME 9.

What do you think of that jellybean story, Bert, huh? It's a real cliff hanger.
Ernie